Sniffing
for
Clues
Collection

Based on the characters created by **SUSAN MEDDAUGH**

HOUGHTON MIFFLIN HARCOURT
Boston New York

Contents

For information about permission to reproduce selections from this book, write to Permissions, Houghton Mifflin Harcourt Publishing Company, 215 Park Avenue South, New York, New York 10003.

ISBN: 978-0-544-34118-0 pa
www.hmhco.com
www.marthathetalkingdog.com

Manufactured in China
SCP 10 9 8 7 6 5 4 3 2 1
4500498668

Martha on the Case

Adaptation by Jamie White
Based on a TV series teleplay written by Matt Steinglass
Based on the characters created by Susan Meddaugh

MARTHA SAYS HELLO

Hi there!

Get ready for . . . action!
Danger! Doggy biscuits!

In other words, get ready
for this book starring me,
Martha the talking dog!

Ever since my owner
Helen fed me her alphabet
soup, I've been able to speak.
And speak and speak . . . No
one's sure how or why,

but the letters in the soup traveled up to my
brain instead of down to my stomach.

Now, as long as I eat my daily bowl of
alphabet soup, I can talk. To my family—
Helen, baby Jake, Mom, Dad, and our nontalking dog, Skits. To Helen's best human
friend, T.D. To anyone who'll listen, really.

Sometimes my family wishes I didn't talk
quite so much. But who can argue with a
talking dog? Besides, my speaking comes
in handy. One night I
witnessed a burglar break

in to our house. No kidding. I saw him with my own eyes. I called 911 and saved the day!

Of course, I can speak to other dogs—and cats, too. But cats can be trouble. Take the time I went to Alice Boxwood's party. I made the mistake of talking to her cat, Nelson. And, well, read on to see what happened . . .

Sit, stay, and hear all about it . . .

Part One
AN INVITATION

It was an ordinary day in Wagstaff City.

Helen and T.D. had eaten lunch outside the yogurt shop. Martha sat in her usual place by their feet, ready to catch any little bite that came her way.

"Yum!" said Martha, still tasting that last piece of burger. "Like I always say, the best seat in the house is under the table."

They were almost ready to go when something happened.

While Helen wasn't looking, T.D. swiped at her plate.

Helen raised her head. She looked at her food. "Okay, where did it go?"

"Where did what go?" T.D. said. "I'm innocent! I didn't do it!"

"Yes, you did," said Helen. "You're guilty."

"No, I'm not. Where's your evidence?"

"Look at my plate," Helen said. "I had one fry. Now I have none. Plus, you have french fry stuck between your teeth."

"Rats!" T.D. said, covering his mouth. "Where?"

Helen smiled. "Actually, I made that up."

"You win!" T.D. said. "I did it. Guilty as charged."

Yes, it was just your ordinary day in Wagstaff City—a boy, a girl, and a talking dog. Then Alice Boxwood appeared.

Alice was Helen and T.D.'s friend. She was also the owner of a sneaky cat named Nelson.

"Hi, guys!" said Alice. "Guess what? You're all invited!"

"To what?" T.D. asked.

"My birthday party!" Alice said, holding up invitations for the three of them.

"NOOOO!" Helen shouted.

"AHHHH!" T.D. screamed at the same time.

"Hooray!" Martha said. "My first party!"

Martha was so excited that she'd forgotten what Helen had told her about Alice's parties. They always ended with a bang. Or a crash! Or a *kaboom!*

When Alice turned three, she tried to blow out her candles. But she leaned in too far. *SPLAT!* The kids got their cake in a surprising way when Alice fell face-first into it.

Two years ago, Alice had a make-your-own-sundae party. But the only thing Alice made was a mess. She tripped into a tray of sundaes. Ice cream splattered everywhere. (This was later known as Alice's *wear*-your-own-sundae party.)

Then last year was the
year of miniature golf. Alice
had a great swing, but her aim was not very
good. Her balls flew in every direction except
the hole. One golf ball hit the windmill on
the next tee and jammed the gears of a water
wheel. The wheel broke away.

"Run for your lives!" T.D. had shouted.

Alice Boxwood's parties were not for the
faint of heart.

"Don't worry," said Alice. "This year I'm having a costume party. Come dressed as your favorite invention."

"My favorite invention?" said Martha. "I'm a huge fan of the sausage. Whoever invented it is a genius! Then there's the chew toy, the comfy chair, and—"

"Great. See you there!" said Alice, walking away.

Helen looked worried. "We'd better dress as bubble wrap," she said.

"Or a suit of armor," T.D. grumbled.

NELSON'S QUESTION

On the day of Alice's party, Helen was still
a little nervous. But Martha couldn't wait.
Her tail wagged in excited circles as she
followed Helen down the street.

"I love my costume," Martha said.
"The doggy door! It's the greatest invention
since meat!"

"Here we are," Helen said, stopping in
front of a house.

Martha's tail stopped wagging.

"Oh, no!" Martha said. "The party is at Alice's *house?*"

"What's wrong?" Helen asked.

Martha was looking at a large, fluffy cat with beady yellow eyes sitting on Alice's front porch.

"Nelson," said Martha with a shudder. "That cat is trouble."

"Come on," said Helen. "The party is in the backyard. You'll have fun. Besides, how much trouble could one little kitty cat be?"

"You don't know Nelson," Martha said. But she followed Helen to the backyard.

The yard was decorated with hot air balloons and other aircraft. The guests were dressed as all kinds of inventions. Alice greeted them in a parachute costume.

"What do you think?" Alice said. "My parents really got into the whole invention thing."

"I'll say," said Martha, looking around. "Helen, is that lipstick over there your cousin Carolina?"

"Yes," said Helen.

Then something on the other side of the
yard caught Martha's attention.

"Wow! That's the biggest hot dog I've ever
seen," she said. "This is my kind of party!"

"Martha!" Helen said. "That's not a real
hot dog. That's T.D."

"He's with the robot clown my parents
hired," Alice said, wincing.

Alice walked to the middle of the yard where everyone could see her.

"Attention, everyone!" she announced. "It's game time! Who wants to play pin-the-tail-on-the-donkey?"

She raised a sharp pin into the air.

"AAAAH!" everyone screamed. Who knew what Alice might do with a sharp object?

"I have a better game," Martha said quickly. "It's called give-the-dog-a-biscuit."

"Phew," said Helen. "Great idea, Martha. How do you play?"

26

Martha told Alice to find a box of
doggy biscuits. Then she explained how
to play.

"Truman, you go first," said Alice. "You're
the brain of the group."

Helen's neighbor Truman stepped
forward. Alice handed him a biscuit
and blindfolded him.

"I can't see a thing," Truman said as Alice
stepped away.

"Perfect," said Martha. In a flash, she
snatched the biscuit from Truman's hand and
gobbled it up.

"A winner!" she cried.

"But I didn't even start yet," Truman said.

"Then let's try again," Martha said. "Another biscuit, please?"

But as soon as Truman had the biscuit in his hand, Martha snatched it and ate it.

Martha ate biscuit after biscuit until all of the biscuits were gone. And still, no one had figured out how the game worked.

"But who won?" T.D. asked.

"You're *all* winners!" Martha said. *"BURP!* Thanks for letting me play."

Martha left the puzzled guests and waddled to a quiet corner of the yard. She found a big stick and began to play with it.

Meow.

Nelson's voice stopped Martha
in midmotion.

"Nelson," she said. "What do you want?"

Meow, Nelson mewed sweetly.

"Yes. Dogs can pick up a lot with
their mouths. So what?"

Meow, meow.

"Prove it? No problem."

Martha picked up a rock with her mouth.

"Phwee?" She spit it out. "I mean, *see?* No problem."

Nelson's yellow eyes twinkled. *Meow?*

"You?" Martha said. "Of course, I could pick you up. Easy."

And that's just what she did.

A CRUMBY SURPRISE

As soon as Martha tried to lift Nelson gently with her teeth, he let out a loud, exaggerated *YOWL!*

Martha quickly dropped him. Nelson was no fun. Martha left him to go inside for a nap, but it wasn't two seconds before all the children gathered around her. Alice's older brother, Ronald, was holding Nelson. *Meow,* Nelson whimpered, looking wounded, as though he were about to faint.

"You shouldn't bite Nelson, Martha," said Helen.

"I didn't. I'm innocent!" Martha said.

Ronald cradled the limp cat in his arms.

"Poor kitty," Ronald cooed. "Look, there's slobber in his fur."

"Well, *you* try putting a cat in *your* mouth and see if you don't get . . ." Martha's voice trailed off. "This doesn't sound good, does it?"

Ronald scowled, and everyone looked
at Martha.

"You're all biased!" Martha said. "You
assume I'm guilty without hearing my side
of the story."

"Martha," Helen said. "I'm sure you
weren't trying to hurt Nelson, but Ronald
would feel better if you stayed in the garage."

"I've been framed!" Martha cried. "I've
been falsely accused. The cat set me up."

Helen walked Martha to the garage. "Look," Helen said, opening the door. "You've had a lot of biscuits. Why don't you take a nap here?"

"All right," Martha snapped. She lay on the garage floor. "I'll nap. But I won't like it! This is totally . . . "

Before she could finish, Martha was fast asleep. Zzzzz.

Back at the party, Alice announced, "Piñata time!"

"An electronic piñata?" T.D. said.

"My dad says it's the latest thing," Alice said. "There's only one problem."

She tapped the piñata with a stick. "YOU WIN!" it said. Pictures of candy danced across the screen.

"The candy's electronic, too," said Alice sadly.

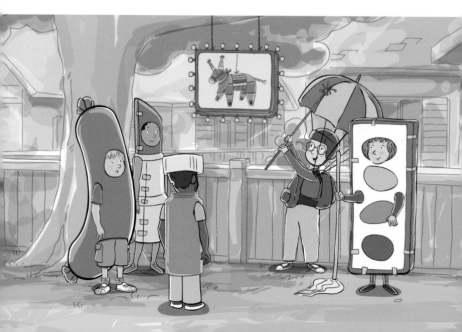

Their game was interrupted by a shout from the kitchen.

"OH, NO!" Mrs. Boxwood exclaimed.

The kids ran inside.

"What's the matter, Mom?" Alice asked.

Standing by the table, Mrs. Boxwood held up Alice's birthday cake.

"Someone ate part of your cake!" Mrs. Boxwood said. "Who could have done this?"

"At least *I* didn't do it this time," said Alice, with relief.

Truman examined the cake. "It's not sliced, and there are no finger marks. It looks like an animal ate it."

"Animal?" Ronald said. "Hmm. I know what happened."

He marched to the garage. The other kids followed.

"Aha!" said Ronald, opening the garage door. "Look what's in front of Martha!"

Martha woke up, yawning. She looked at the floor. "Oh, hey! Are those cake crumbs? Yum!"

She licked them up.

"Admit it," said Ronald. "You're guilty. You ate my sister's cake!"

Martha raised her head. "CAKE! Where?"

"Don't act innocent," Ronald said.

"She *is* innocent," said Helen. "She wasn't anywhere near it."

"There's only one way to find out the truth," said Ronald. "Put Martha on trial! In a trial, you *have* to tell the truth."

He looked through some tools and found a mallet. "This will be my gavel. I'll be the judge."

"Oh no, you won't," Alice said, grabbing the gavel. "We need someone who's not biased to be the judge."

"Biased? *Me?*" Ronald said.

"Yes, *you,*" said Alice. "You've already made up your mind that Martha did it."

Alice handed the gavel to Truman. "Truman, you be the judge. The rest of us will be the jury. We'll decide if Martha is guilty or innocent."

"Jury duty?" said Carolina. "Yuck! I came for a party."

"Really? I came for cake," said Martha.

MARTHA INTERRUPTS

Excuse me. I have to interrupt the story.
We're about to get to the part where I wasn't
allowed to talk much. I'd like to make up
for it now.

  We all sat in the backyard for the trial.
I'll sit for lots of things. Cake,
for example. Instead I was
sitting next to Truman,
the judge, who kept
telling me to be quiet.

In front of us, the jury—Alice, Carolina, and Helen—sat on two picnic benches.

"Order in the court!" Truman shouted. *BANG, BANG!* He slammed his gavel on the picnic table.

"No cake *and* no talking?" I said. "This isn't a party. This is a cruel joke!"

"Shhh," said Truman. "Ronald, present your evidence."

Ronald paced in front of the jury.

"First, we all know that cats are better than dogs," he said. "Dogs have fleas. Dogs stink."

What was Ronald talking about? I smell *great*.

"I object!" I said. "I don't stink! I smell different every day. It all depends on what I've rolled in. Today I smell like old shoes and banana peels. Fragrant and delightful!"

"Quiet, Martha!" Truman shouted. Then he said, "Ronald, that's not evidence."

"Well, it's what's wrong with dogs," Ronald said.

"Evidence isn't your opinion. Evidence is something that would help prove Martha is guilty of the crime," said Truman.

"Evidence?" Ronald repeated. "Like the cake crumbs?"

"Precisely."

"There were cake crumbs around Martha," Ronald said. "That proves she ate the cake. It's an open and shut case."

T.D. leaped to his feet. "Open and shut is right! The garage door was shut. How could a dog open it?"

"That's right. No hands!" I added.

"Then there's the crumbs," said T.D. "You like crumbs, don't you, Martha?"

"I do," I said. "I call them floor food."

"Why would Martha leave all those crumbs?" T.D. asked the court. "Answer? She wouldn't! Someone wanted Martha to look guilty. Someone had it in for Martha from the beginning. Someone like . . . NELSON!"

Nelson sat on the ground in front of the jury, looking fluffy and harmless. Drat him.

"Nelson?" Ronald said. "How could he do it? Look at him. He's so cute."

"Que lindo," Carolina cooed, agreeing with Ronald.

Cute? I thought. Was I the only one who saw through his act?

"Hang on, T.D.," said Ronald. "You said a dog couldn't open a door. How could a cat?"

I wondered what T.D. could say now. He paused for a moment, and then he said, "Maybe the door *wasn't* opened!"

"What do you mean?" Ronald asked.

"The cat ate the cake," said T.D. "The problem was finding someone to take the blame. Here's how it went . . ."

Trust me: you won't believe how it went! I'll let you get back to the story to find out.

THE VERDICT

"Nelson is not your ordinary cat," T.D. said to the jury. "His skills will surprise you. After he ate the cake, he knew just what to do.

"He connected a wire to the ceiling and climbed up it. Then he took out his drill and opened an air duct. He crawled inside. Once Nelson was above the garage, he grabbed his blowtorch—"

"Nelson has a *blowtorch?*" Alice asked.

"Just let me tell the story," T.D. said. "He cut a hole in the garage ceiling.

"Then he slipped through the hole and quietly landed next to Martha. He wiped his whiskers and the cake crumbs fell to the floor."

"But how did he escape?" Helen asked.

"Through the window," T.D. said. "Nelson ran a wire from the garage window to a tree. He zipped across it.

"So you see," T.D. continued, "the garage door never had to be opened at all."

Ronald shook his head. "That's the most ridiculous thing I've ever heard. Martha is guilty. She ate the cake!"

Suddenly there was a pitiful sound from Nelson. *Meow-OW.*

"What's wrong with Nelson?" Martha asked.

Nelson looked queasy.

"Nelson!" Ronald cried. He watched his cat gag, and then . . .

"Yuck! What is it?" Carolina asked.

"It's a birthday candle," Alice said. "*You* ate my cake, Nelson?"

Nelson wobbled. He swayed. He fell on his face.

"My poor baby!" Ronald said, scooping him up.

"You should take him to the vet," Martha suggested. "Maybe he ate more candles."

"Good thinking," said Alice.

Just then, Mrs. Boxwood walked into the yard. "I have another cake!" she sang, placing a box on the picnic table.

"Mom, we have to bring Nelson to
the vet," Ronald said. "I'll explain on the way."

"Oh dear," said Mrs. Boxwood. She shook
her head as she followed Ronald to the car.
"Alice's parties are always an adventure."

As they left, the rest of the party eyed the cake.

"Cake!" Martha said. "Look at my tail go! I call this my cake dance."

"Order!" said Truman. "You're still on trial. Has the jury reached a verdict?"

"Not guilty!" the jury cheered.

"You're acquitted, Martha. You're exonerated of all charges," Truman said.

"Are you speaking English?" Martha asked.

"I mean, you're innocent," said Truman.

"In that case," said Alice, raising the gavel into the air. "I declare this trial . . . closed!"

She slammed the gavel down.

"NOOOO!" Helen and T.D. screamed at the same time.

"Hooray!" said Martha, licking frosting from her face. "What a party!"

MARTHA SPEAKS AGAIN

Thanks to Nelson, my first party wasn't *purr*fect. But even though I was put on trial, I still had fun. (Oh, and don't worry about Nelson. He's feeling better.)

Helen and I never did figure out how the crumbs got in the garage. But as we left Alice's, I noticed something.

A wire ran from her garage window to a tree.
It might have been a clothesline. Or . . . is
Nelson really an expert thief?

Nah!

Oh, well. I guess it'll just have to remain
a mystery.

Keep reading for another mystery. See how
I help crack this case!

Part Two

NO DOGS ALLOWED

I'm a pretty happy dog, Martha thought. But I'd be happier without three things: leashes, baths, and NO DOGS ALLOWED signs.

Martha stared at the Squiggy Piggy Mart's door. It had a picture of a dog with a slash through it.

"It's just rude," Martha said.

"You know dogs aren't allowed inside. It's the rules," said Helen. She tied Martha's leash to a parking meter. "I'll be right back."

Helen patted Martha's head and walked into the store.

"We should move to France!" Martha shouted. "French dogs get to go everywhere! They live like kings! Kings, I tell you!"

Hmph, Martha thought. *This is unfair. I'm not happy. Nothing could make me happy. Nothing! Not even—*

Martha smiled. "Hey, is that a cookie?"

In a stroller next to her, a baby held a mushy cookie.

"Bow-wow," said the baby.

"Yes," said Martha. "Doggies say 'bow-wow.'"

The baby pointed a crumb-covered finger at Martha.

"Let me clean you up," Martha said. She licked cookie crumbs off the baby's hand.

"Ahem," said the baby's mother.

Martha looked up. "Oh, hi! That's one smart baby you've got there. Tasty, too!"

The mother quickly pushed the stroller away.

"Bye, baby!" Martha called after them.

A car pulled up behind her, and two men stepped out. One was tall. The other was short. They both looked pretty scruffy.

Wow, Martha thought. *Those men look like they hate baths as much as I do.*

"Out of my way, mutt," said the tall one. He put coins into the meter.

"This job is going to be a piece of cake," said the short one.

Cake? Mmm, Martha thought.

"It'll be like taking candy from a baby," said the other.

"Ahh, candy," said Martha. "Wait! Take? Baby? Oh, no! That poor baby!"

The men headed in the same direction as the stroller.

"Don't worry, baby!" Martha hollered. "No one's going to take your candy while I'm around!"

Martha ran after the men, but the leash stopped her short.

PLUMBING FOR FLOWERS

Helen walked out of the Squiggy Piggy Mart
with a bag of groceries.

"Helen!" Martha cried. "Quick, untie me!"

Helen untied Martha's leash from
the meter. "What's the rush?"

"We've got to stop a crime!" Martha said,
taking off.

"WHOA!" Helen shouted. "*I'm* supposed
to be walking *you!* What's going on?"

"I overheard two men discussing a plot,"
Martha said. "They mentioned candy . . .
and babies . . . and cake! We have to act fast."

"But—" Helen said.

Martha stopped at the store the men
had entered. She peered inside.

"I don't see anyone. We're too late!"
she wailed. "Those men stole all the cake and
probably that poor baby's candy, too!"

Then Martha spotted the men in a corner
of the store. They spotted her, too.

"Duck!" said Martha.

"Martha!" said Helen. "Nobody robbed
this store. It closed last month. Remember?"

The store door swung open. Martha
gulped.

"Are you looking for something, kid?" the
tall man asked.

"No," said Helen, blushing. "My silly dog
thought the store was being robbed. But you
must be opening a new store. What kind?"

"Plumbing," said one.

"Flowers," said the other at the same time.

The men glared at each other.

"Plumbing flowers?" Helen asked.

"It's a flower shop that sells plumbing stuff," the tall man mumbled. "It's easier to keep your flowers watered that way. Now beat it, kid."

The two men went back into the shop and slammed the door.

"Geesh. He'll need to work on his customer service skills," Helen said. "Let's go."

"But I'm positive those guys are criminals,"

said Martha. "They're *very* suspicious. I don't trust them. Plus, they said they were going to take candy from a baby!"

"They weren't talking about a real baby," said Helen. "That's a figure of speech. You know, an expression? It's a funny way of saying something."

"Huh?" Martha said.

"If you say something will be like taking candy from a baby, you mean it'll be easy."

Martha was not convinced. "Plumbing-flower shop?" she said. "Doesn't that seem suspicious?"

Helen shrugged. "It's possible."

"It's also possible they're plotting a crime." Martha walked in circles, and as she walked, her leash wound around Helen's legs. "We have to trip them up!" she said, and took off running.

But the only one who tripped was Helen.

"Whoops," said Martha. "Sorry."

MARTHA HERE AGAIN

Can you believe that Helen didn't think those men were up to no good? It was obvious to me, but who listens to the dog?

Helen's friend T.D. came over for a game, and because we were playing catch, another member of the family joined us. Skits can't talk, but he's never met a flying object he didn't want to catch.

T.D. threw a flying disk and Skits leaped up and caught it in midair. He almost landed on me.

"Hey! Watch where you're going!" I said.

Woof, Skits barked.

"What nerve! Of course I could have caught it," I said. Sometimes I have to remind Skits that *I'm* the alpha dog. "I'm busy thinking. I'm trying to uncover a plot."

Woof, woof. Skits pawed at the ground.

"No," I explained. "Not a plot of land. A 'plot' like a plan. I think the guys I saw are plotting to commit a crime."

"Believe me," Helen said. "The only thing those guys are plotting is how to open a plumbing-flower shop."

But T.D. said, "I think Martha might be right. Something smells fishy."

"It's probably me," I said. "I rolled in something earlier. You like it? I thought it was frog, but maybe it was fish."

"It's an expression," said T.D. "If you
say something smells fishy, you think it's
suspicious. Those guys might be plotting to
rob a bank or—"

T.D. was interrupted by news on the radio.

"This just in!" the DJ announced. "Police
are on the lookout for safecracker Louie
Kablooie and his accomplice, Jimmy Gimme.
The criminals are believed to be in the area,
plotting a robbery."

"Could it be the men we saw?" Helen said.

"It *has* to be," I said. "I knew I was right!"
People are so slow to pick up what a dog
knows right away.

"I need to see those men for myself,"
said T.D.

And before you could say "plumbing
flowers," Helen, T.D., and I were next to the
empty store. We watched the men talk inside.
The tall one pointed to something on a map.
The other nodded.

"Those two are Kablooie and Gimme,"
I whispered. "I'm positive. Look! They're
probably pointing at the jewelry store on that
map. That must be what they plan to rob!"

"Then why are they in an empty store
across the street from it?" Helen asked.

"I know!" said T.D. "I saw it in a movie."
He took out his drawing pad. "They're going
to go into the empty store's basement.
They'll dig a tunnel under the street and into
the jewelry store's basement. Then they'll
crack the safe and steal the jewels.
It's easy pickings."

"Pickings?" I said. "There are fruit trees in the basement?"

Helen and T.D. threw up their arms. "It's an expression!" they shouted.

"People have too many expressions!" I said. "Well, how do we stop them?"

"Simple," said T.D. "I'll sneak inside and

redraw their map. Instead of digging into the
jewelry store, they'll dig into the public pool.
When they hit water, they'll slosh back into
the tunnel. Then—POP!—they'll burst out of
a manhole. We'll be waiting there with
the cops!"

"One problem," Helen said. "The pool is two blocks away. They'd have to dig for weeks."

T.D. said, "I'm willing to wait."

"Maybe we should tell the police," Helen said.

"Then we'll need proof," I said. "You know, evidence? Something to convince the police that those guys are crooks."

Helen jumped to her feet. "I have an idea!"

And boy, did she!

SNOOPS

Back at Helen's house, Martha and T.D. watched Helen search for something in her bedroom.

"I know it's here somewhere," Helen said. "Martha and I just used it to make our own music video."

Finally, she found what she wanted.

"Ta-da!" said Helen, holding up a toy. "We'll catch the thieves with this! It's my Sing-and-Go karaoke machine."

"What are you going to do?" T.D. asked. "Sing until they surrender?"

Helen gave T.D. a hard look. "This has a built-in video camera. If those guys do anything suspicious, we'll record it. We'll show the tape to the police as proof that they're criminals."

"Good idea!" said T.D.

"Are you sure you want to be my accomplices?" Helen asked.

"Isn't an accomplice a person who helps somebody do something wrong?" Martha asked.

"Well, snooping *is* wrong," said Helen.

"But we're snooping to stop a crime," T.D. said. "We're more like *partners* than accomplices."

Helen smiled. "Okay then—partners?"

"Partners!" they said together.

Soon Martha, Helen, and T.D. were spying on the men once again. This time, they hid behind a mailbox next to the empty store.

Helen videotaped the suspects. She filmed them looking at a map. She filmed them watching the jewelry store.

"Are we missing anything?" asked Helen.

Martha's head popped in front of the lens.

"ME!" she said, posing. "Be sure to get my good side."

"Martha!" Helen and T.D. groaned.

Helen looked back at the store. "Uh-oh! They're leaving. Quick, hide!"

Crouched behind the mailbox, they

watched the men get into their car. The car
sped off with a screech!

"That's all the proof we'll get,"
Martha said. "Let's take it to the police."

The police station was only a short
walk away. Martha, Helen, and T.D. went
straight to the chief.

"Louie Kablooie, eh?" the police chief said.

"This isn't like when you thought robots had taken over the toy store, is it?"

"No, sir," said T.D. "But in my defense, those robot costumes were really good."

"We have proof," said Helen, holding up the karaoke machine. "Take a look. It's Kablooie and his accomplice, all right."

Helen pressed play.

But instead of Louie Kablooie and Jimmy Gimme, Martha and Helen popped onto the screen. "OH, WHERE, OH, WHERE HAS MY LITTLE DOG GONE?" they sang. "OH, WHERE, OH—"

"NO! That's not it!" Helen said, covering her eyes.

"I've seen enough," said the police chief.

"Wait! You'll miss my big finish," Martha said.

On the screen, Martha rapped. "OH, WHERE CAN SHE BUH-BUH-BUH-*BE!*"

Helen grabbed the Sing-and-Go. "I must have hit the wrong track. The criminals are on here somewhere."

"Sure," said the chief, walking them to the door. "Don't worry. I'll check it out."

Outside the station, Helen sighed. "I don't think he believed us."

"Sure, he did," said Martha. "And I think he loved my big finish!"

"Well, there's only one way to know for sure," said T.D. "Let's go back to the empty store. We'll see if the police chief arrests those men."

Helen and Martha nodded.

They all walked back to the store.

Inside, the men had returned to their earlier positions. The tall one was watching the jewelry store. The other was taking notes. Neither one of them heard the back door creak open.

"How's it going?" said a deep voice behind them.

"Aah!" the waiting men hollered. They spun around.

"Oh, it's just you," said the tall one. "All is quiet."

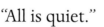

"Keep watching," said the police chief. "All evidence suggests that Kablooie is planning to rob that jewelry store today."

"He'd better hurry," the short man said. "It's three o'clock. An armored car is coming to pick up the jewels at four."

"If Kablooie strikes, we'll be ready for him," the police chief said. "Oh, and try not to be so obvious. A couple kids spotted you. They think you're Kablooie and Gimme!"

Hiding behind the mailbox, Martha, Helen, and T.D. watched the three men laugh as if they'd just heard the funniest joke.

"Why isn't the chief arresting them?"
Martha said. "How much proof does
he need?"

Helen shrugged. "It's in the hands of the
police now. Let's go home."

T.D. and Helen walked away. But Martha
stayed behind.

"I can't let those guys rob the jewelry
store," she said. "I have to do something!"

HOWWWL!

As the clock ticked, the two men waited.

"Kablooie's going to walk right into our trap," the tall man said. "As long as things stay nice and quiet." But at that moment . . .

"LOUIE KABLOOIE, COME OUT WITH YOUR HANDS UP!" Martha shouted into the Sing-and-Go microphone. "I REPEAT: COME OUT WITH YOUR HANDS—"

Her paw accidentally hit a wrong button.

"OH, WHERE, OH, WHERE CAN SHE BUH-BUH-BUH-*BE!*" came out instead.

Martha fumbled with the machine. "Ugh, paws!"

"Yes, press *pause!*" said a voice.

Martha looked up. It was the short man. The tall one stood next to him. They looked even angrier than before.

"We need to talk," said the tall man.

"Bow-wow?" she said.

"Nice try, talking dog," said the short one. "I'm Officer O'Reilly. Minetti here is my partner. We're trying to catch thieves robbing that jewelry store."

He showed Martha two mug shots.

Uh-oh. The real Kablooie and Gimme look nothing like these cops, Martha thought.

"Gee, I'm sorry I was suspicious of you, officers," Martha said. "I feel awful."

"Just stay out of our way," Minetti said. "Kablooie should be here any minute. The last thing we need is some rapping mutt messing things up."

And with that, they walked away. As she stood alone on the sidewalk, Martha's ears drooped.

The men returned to the store. They checked the time.

Tick, TOCK! The clock struck four.

The men looked at the jewelry store.

"There's the armored car," said Minetti, looking through binoculars. "But where's Kablooie? I guess we were wrong about him."

"He must be hitting another jewelry store," O'Reilly said.

Minetti packed up his things. "Our work here is done."

Martha decided to go home. She picked up the karaoke machine in her mouth.

Not only did I blow the case, but I'm getting Helen's toy all slobbery, too, she thought.

Just then, the slam of a heavy metal door caught her attention. Martha looked up to see the armored truck. It was still in front of the jewelry store. A security guard had stepped out of it.

That guy looks familiar, she thought.

Martha's jaw dropped. The Sing-and-Go fell to the ground.

"Sizzling sausages!" she cried. "That's no security guard! It's Louie Kablooie!"

Martha raced to the empty store. She looked inside.

"Oh, no! The cops are gone!" she said. "What do I do?"

Martha thought fast. She needed help. She threw back her head and opened her mouth.

Ahwooooo! Her howl traveled to every corner of Wagstaff City.

In a bathtub, a boxer raised his soapy head. On a porch step, a Dalmatian perked up his ears. All across town dogs heard Martha's howl. They streamed out their doors and into the streets. Soon they were one large pack running toward Martha's call for help.

103

My dog friends better hurry, Martha thought.
*Kablooie and Gimme are already leaving the store
with bags. They're about to make their getaway!*

"See?" Kablooie said. "Piece of cake."

"But boss, I didn't get any cake. I only got
jewels," Gimme replied.

"It's an expression, you nitwit!"
Kablooie said. "Let's get these bags into
the truck!"

The sound of barking began to fill the air.

"What's all that racket?" Kablooie said,
reaching for the truck's door.

WOOF! ARF! YIP! The barks grew louder.

A mob of dogs began to surround the truck.

"Yikes!" said Kablooie, dropping his bag. He raised his hands into the air.

"We're trapped!" said Gimme. He dropped his bag, too.

"Way to go, dogs!" Martha shouted. "Keep Kablooie and his accomplice in line. Grab their bags. We'll need them as evidence."

Two dogs dragged the bags away with their teeth.

Down the street, sirens blared. Red lights flashed. The police chief's car arrived at the scene.

"You two are going to jail for a long time," the chief said.

"That's just an expression, right?" said Gimme.

"Nope," said Martha. "You're really going to jail!"

"And it's all thanks to—" The police chief puffed up his chest and rapped, "MUH-MUH-MUH-*MARTHA!*"

Martha wagged her tail. "Now that's what I call a big finish!"

MARTHA SAYS GOODBYE

Just for now!

It was a proud moment for us dogs. The police chief thanked me. Even Officer O'Reilly and Officer Minetti seemed impressed.

That night, I watched the news with Helen.

"Tonight's top story," said the reporter. "Police caught

expert safecracker Louie Kablooie and his accomplice, Jimmy Gimme. The police were aided by a secret partner. They wouldn't reveal the identity, saying she's only known by her code name: Martha."

Helen didn't say a word. But she gave me an extra belly rub.

Now, one thing is for sure. The police station will never have a NO DOGS ALLOWED sign. And that makes me one happy dog!

GLOSSARY

How many words do you remember from the story?

accomplice: a person who helps another do something wrong

biased: having an assumption that somebody is guilty or innocent without hearing his or her side of the story

evidence: something used to prove a person (or a certain talking dog) committed a crime

expression: a figure of speech or funny way of saying something

guilty: responsible for a crime or wrongdoing

innocent: free from legal guilt

plot: a secret plan for committing a crime

positive: certain, sure

proof: evidence, something that convinces a person of a crime committed

suspicious: distrustful, questionable

witness: to see a fact or event

Okay, detectives! Break out your binoculars. How many words do you spy? Using the clues, fill in the missing words. Then circle the words in the puzzle below.

```
A   W   B   A   G   J   U   R   Y
T   R   I   A   L   U   M   S   N
P   L   A   T   N   D   I   E   C
O   L   S   O   F   G   L   L   A
C   R   O   O   K   E   U   R   T
T   J   O   T   H   O   W   L   Q
S   R   R   T   F   I   S   H   Y
P   A   R   T   N   E   R   S   G
Y   E   V   I   D   E   N   C   E
```

CLUES:

1. If you say something smells _ _ _ _ _, you think it's suspicious.

2. Kablooie came up with a _ _ _ _ to rob the jewelry store.

3. As the _ _ _ _ _, Truman was in charge of the trial and yelled "ORDER!" a lot.

4. Martha, Helen, and T.D. worked together as _ _ _ _ _ _ _ _.

5. Ronald put Martha on _ _ _ _ _ to see if she was guilty or innocent of the crime.

Now find these bonus words!

bag, bias, cat, cop, crook, guilt, Helen, howl, spy, T.D., evidence, jury, true, proof

ANSWERS:

1. fishy **2.** plot **3.** judge **4.** partners **5.** trial

ALPHABET SOUP

Oops! Someone knocked over Martha's alphabet soup. Unscramble the soup letters to form words from the story and glossary. To find out who spilled the soup, unscramble the underlined letters.

1. Gimme, who was Kablooie's nitwit **EAPCMCOL<u>I</u>C,** helped him rob the jewelry store.

2. "Easy pickings" is an **NSI<u>E</u>SOXREP.**

3. If Martha had eaten Alice's cake, she'd be **<u>I</u>YGTLU.**

4. A plumbing-flower shop seems **OPSIS<u>C</u>USIU.**

5. Ronald was **<u>A</u>IDEBS.** He thought Martha ate the cake without hearing all the facts.

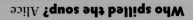

Who spilled the soup? Alice

ANSWERS:
1. accomplice **2.** expression **3.** guilty
4. suspicious **5.** biased

Detective Dog

Adaptation by Jamie White
Based on TV series teleplays
written by Raye Lankford and Peter K. Hirsch
Based on characters created by Susan Meddaugh

Part One
POOCH ON PATROL

A dog's life is never dull. Especially when you're a talking dog like me, Martha!

Ever since Helen fed me her alphabet soup, I've been able to speak. And speak and speak . . . No one's sure how or why, but the letters in the soup traveled up to my brain instead of down to my stomach.

Now as long as I eat my daily bowl of alphabet soup, I can talk. To my family— Helen, baby Jake, Mom, Dad, and Skits, who only speaks Dog. To Helen's best human friend, T.D. To anyone who'll listen.

117

Sometimes my family wishes I didn't talk quite so much. But my speaking has come in handy when fighting crime. Like the time I called 911 to catch a burglar. Or when I became a K-9 cop!

Oh, sure, I'd once thought a stakeout was the butcher shop's version of takeout, and the only things I'd pursued were squirrels and garbage trucks. But that was before Helen, Skits, and I bumped into Officer O'Reilly in town. He was with a dog!

Skits and I greeted him with a nice-to-meet-you sniff. But the dog just stood there. "What's the matter with him?" I asked.

"He's on duty," said Officer O'Reilly. "Rascal's part of our K-9 unit."

"You mean he's a police dog?" I asked.

"Yup," he replied. "We're just finishing our beat. Unfortunately, my partner and I are going to be in different cities tomorrow." He puffed out his chest. "There's a big case in Chicago. They need a smart cop to help them crack it."

"You're going to Chicago?" I asked.

"Uh . . . not me," he mumbled, glancing down at Rascal. "I'll be stuck patrolling alone for the next few days."

"You don't have to patrol alone," I said. "I could patrol with you."

Officer O'Reilly didn't look too sure. "Really?"

"Why not?" I asked. "When you patrol, you go around making sure everything is okay, right?"

"Right," he said.

"I'm great at patrolling!" I said. "I patrol my yard all the time. Watch." I paced the sidewalk, looking left and right. "See? I'm patrolling. Nope, no criminals here."

Officer O'Reilly rubbed his chin. "I don't know. Being a K-9 officer requires special training."

"But I'm the police force's secret weapon," I reminded him. "I brought in Louie Kablooie and Jimmy Gimme Moore. And the dogs that were robbing the butcher's!"

To convince him, I showed off my best tricks. I sat, stayed, and played dead. I even begged. "Please? Please let me be a cop! Please please please please PLEASE!"

"Oh, all right," Officer O'Reilly sighed. "Report to the station tomorrow. We start walking the beat at nine o'clock sharp."

Hot dog!

BUGGING OUT

How does a dog learn to be a top K-9 cop? By watching TV's coolest crime-fighting canine, Courageous Collie Carlo! Sigh. He's so dreamy.

I was in the middle of my fourth episode when Helen interrupted. "Can't I watch my show now?" she asked.

"Sorry," I replied. "No time for idle television viewing. I've got to be prepared for my beat tomorrow."

On TV, the officer was making an arrest. "POLICE! FREEZE!" he ordered. *So that's how it's done,* I thought.

All day and night, I watched TV cops bust bad guys. They shouted "POLICE! FREEZE!" 102 more times. Helen had counted.

"TV is not going to teach you how to be a police dog," she groaned.

"How can you say that? Look what I've learned already!" I said, looking tough.

POLICE! FREEZE!

"Yeah, but none of that stuff ever happens. Like that!" said Helen. On TV, a detective had just discovered smuggled pineapples on a train. "No one smuggles stuff into Wagstaff City."

"Smuggling means you sneak something in that isn't supposed to be there, right?" I said. "So maybe people are smuggling things into Wagstaff City all the time."

"I hope not," said Helen. "Especially if it's food. That would be really bad."

I imagined train cars bursting with burgers, hot dogs, and steaks. A real gravy train. Next stop—Martha's belly! "What could ever be bad about food?" I asked dreamily.

"It could be bad if a bug was hiding in it," said Helen.

"What could an itty-bitty bug do?"

Helen looked serious. "Eat all the crops. Or the forest. Especially if there were lots of bugs."

"That's awful!" I agreed.

Helen yawned and rose to go to bed. "Like I said, it'd never happen in Wagstaff City."

"But what if it did?"

"It won't," said Helen, walking away.

"How can you be sure?" I called after her.
But she left me to worry. "Just think, Skits,"
I said. "There could be smuggled food out
there right now!" I snuggled into my chair.
"I don't know how I'll ever be able to go to
slee—*ZZZZZZZZZ*."

OFFICER MARTHA

The next thing I knew, the sun was shining and I was wearing a police uniform. I was . . . Officer Martha! Oh, yeah. You got that right.

I was a dog on the prowl, cruising the mean city streets in my patrol car. I had a nose for trouble and sniffed out crime by, uh, sniffing. All day, I went above and beyond the smell of duty. Then I hit the doughnut shop with my partner, O'Reilly.

But being a cop wasn't all flashy lights and jelly doughnuts. It was cream-filled doughnuts too. Oh, and bad guys.

That morning, I'd spotted a nervous-looking man in an alley. He'd just stepped out of his truck when I approached him.

"Got any smuggled food in there?" I asked.

The man scoffed. "In Wagstaff City?"

"Oh, right," I said. "Silly me. Have a good day!"

But as I walked away, I heard a loud munching sound. I turned around. The man had opened the back of his truck. It was packed with pineapples! And the munching noise seemed to be coming from inside them!

Within seconds, a gang of bugs chewed their way out of the fruit and took to the sky.

"Let's get cracking," snarled their leader. They swooped down onto a field, clearing crops like a giant lawnmower.

Next they hit the neighborhoods and chomped down all the trees. From our yard, my family watched helplessly below a cloud of sawdust. "I was wrong!" cried Helen. "People do smuggle things into Wagstaff City!"

The bugs buzzed off into the distance.

"Martha, look!" Helen exclaimed. "They're swarming Granny's soup factory!"

I watched in horror as the factory began to disappear. How would I say "POLICE! FREEZE!" without soup? How would I say anything?!

"NOOOOOOOOOOOOOOO!" I yelled.

That was when I woke up from my nightmare.

I padded into the kitchen and stretched just as Helen zoomed around the corner. She slammed into me.

"Oops!" she said.

"POLICE! FREEZE!" I shouted.

Helen grinned. "Is there a problem, Officer?"

"Oh, no problem," I said. "Except for a little *speeding!*"

"Sorry," she said, walking slower. "I'm running late for school."

I gave her my sternest look. "I'm going to have to give you a citation."

"Citation?" asked Helen. "You mean, like a piece of paper that says I broke the law? Like a speeding ticket?"

"Afraid so," I said. Then I remembered dogs can't write. Darn paws! "Uh, grab a notepad and write your citation down, would you? Your fine is five bones."

"I'm guessing you don't mean five dollars," said Helen.

"Nope. Five tasty biscuit bones."

Helen added them to Mom's shopping list. Duty done, I yawned.

"What's the matter?" Helen asked. "Up late fighting crime, Officer Martha?"

"I couldn't sleep," I said, pacing. "I was worrying about smuggled food."

"Martha," said Helen slowly, "there's no smuggling in Wagstaff City."

"But what if there were?"

Helen giggled.

"This is serious!" I said. "The security of our food is at stake."

"It sure is," said Helen, looking at something behind me. I spun around to catch Skits about to eat my soup.

"POLICE! FREEZE!" I said. "Step away from the bowl!"

A police dog's job is never done.

THE SMELL
OF DUTY

At nine o'clock, Officer O'Reilly and I began walking our beat. I told him what was on my mind.

"Smuggling?" he said. "Never happens in Wagstaff City."

"How can you be sure?" I asked.

"Because planes and boats from other countries don't come here," he answered.

I thought this over as we reached the seaport.
A crane was unloading crates from a ship while
the captain and his first mate looked on.

"Morning," said Officer O'Reilly, tipping his
hat to them.

I sniffed the air. "Wait a minute! I smell a rat."

The captain looked nervous, but Officer O'Reilly smiled. "Of course you do," he said. "We're at the dock. It's loaded with rats."

"No," I said. "I mean, something doesn't smell right. It smells like . . . rutabagas."

"R-rutabagas?" the captain stuttered. "Oh, uh, not around here. We don't have those."

Oh yeah? I thought. *Then why is that rat behind you carrying a . . . RUTABAGA?!*

My ears perked up. *And what's that munching sound?* I wondered. But there was no time to find out. I pounced in front of the rat. "POLICE! FREEZE!"

"Squeak!" went the criminal. It fled across the dock, but I was right on its tail.

"Martha, leave it!" cried Officer O'Reilly.

The rat scurried under a forklift moving a crate. I leaped over it. At the sight of me, the driver's mouth dropped. The forklift swerved. And—*CRASH!*—the crate smashed to the dock.

"Officer Martha! Heel!" shouted Officer O'Reilly.

The three men chased me, but I wouldn't stop tailing that rat.

142

Suddenly, the rat dropped the rutabaga and darted into the crack of a door. "Come out with your hands—I mean, paws—up!" I ordered.

Officer O'Reilly and the others limped up behind me. "Martha!" he said. "There's nothing in there."

"You're right," I said. "It's in his pocket!"

Officer O'Reilly turned as purple as a rutabaga. He yanked my collar. "I have to apologize for my partner," he said. "It's her first day on the beat. Come on, Martha. Let's go."

"But I'm telling you," I said as we walked away, "something smells fishy!"

"Of course it's fishy," he snapped. "You're by the river. The river is full of fish."

"Not that kind of fishy."

But Officer O'Reilly just shook his head.

BYE-BYE, BONES

"Fired?" I cried. "You can't fire me."

The chief frowned at me. "I have no choice," he said. "K-9 cops can't chase rats on the beat. It's a matter of security. People could've been hurt."

"But I wasn't chasing the rat!" I protested. "I was chasing the food the rat was carrying."

"K-9 officers don't eat on the beat either," said Officer O'Reilly.

"I wasn't going to eat it," I said. "It's a root vegetable, after all. It's not a sausage. I was going to inspect it."

The men exchanged doubtful glances.

"Come on," I pleaded. "You're not really going to fire me, are you?"

Oh, but they did.

· · · · ·

"I can't believe I got fired, Skits," I said. "How many jobs have I had? Fire dog, radio host, telemarketer . . . I've never been fired from any of them."

I bet Helen won't pay her speeding ticket when she finds out I'm not a cop anymore, I thought. *Bye-bye, bones.*

Just then, a truck drove past us. I sniffed.

"Hey!" I said, bolting up. "It's that smell again."

Woof? barked Skits.

"The smell from the docks," I explained. "It's coming from that truck. Follow me!"

Skits and I tracked the scent into town. It led us to an alley littered with trash cans.

We crept closer. "The captain!" I gasped as the truck's doors opened. "Quick, Skits! Hide!"

We dove into a pile of trash. Just a few feet away, the captain and first mate met by the back of the truck.

"That dog almost blew our cover," said the captain.

   "Yeah," said his partner. "I thought we were done for when she nosed out that rutabaga."

   "Lucky for us," said the captain, "people think there's no smuggling in Wagstaff City."

   "Heh-heh," the men laughed.

   "Skits," I whispered. "Those rutabagas might be risky! We've got tell the police!"

REPORTING RISKY RUTABAGAS

At the police station, the chief and Officer O'Reilly looked weary.

"Thanks for the tip," said the chief. "Run on home now, Martha."

No way, I thought. *If those crooks aren't stopped, who knows what they'll smuggle next? Tons of turnips? Boatloads of beets? Countless crates of cabbage?! Blech.*

"NO!" I cried. "Something smells rotten, I tell you!"

He pinched his nose. "Maybe it's you."

"Oh, uh, that," I mumbled. "I had to take cover in some garbage. Listen! THERE'S SOMETHING WRONG WITH THOSE RUTABAGAS!"

"Okay, okay!" the chief sighed. "O'Reilly, go check it out or she'll never stop hounding us."

"I am not a hound," I said, offended. "But I am part pit bull."

Officer O'Reilly shook his head. "Not *hound* as in a dog breed. *Hound* as in you're bugging us."

"That's it!" I cried. "Bugs! They're in the rutabagas. I heard them chewing!"

I ran out the door.

Skits and Officer O'Reilly followed me back
to the alley. Sure enough, the truck was still
there.

The captain and first mate met with a
jumpy-looking guy. We couldn't hear what
they were saying. But we could see the captain
open the back of his truck. Inside were oodles
of rutabagas!

"Well, what do you know?" Officer
O'Reilly whispered.

Why isn't he arresting them? I wondered. *What's he waiting for?*

Then he turned to me. "Ready, partner?"

My tail wagged in excitement. "Really? I get to say it?"

Officer O'Reilly nodded.

In one leap, I popped out from behind the trash can. "POLICE!" I shouted. "FREEZE!"

The men jumped in surprise. Their rutabaga-smuggling days were over, thanks to . . . Officer Martha! Give that dog a bone.

The next morning, Officer O'Reilly apologized to me as we left the station. "Sorry I didn't believe you."

"It's okay," I said.

"If those bugs had gotten loose, no telling what damage they could've done," he said. "You deserve a medal."

"A medal would be nice, but I can think of something better," I hinted. Because what's the next best thing to taking a bite out of crime? Taking a bite out of a sweet, tasty doughnut.

Later, I told Helen all about it. "Officer O'Reilly said it was the perfect reward for protecting the security of our entire food chain."

Woof? barked Skits.

"*Security* means keeping something safe," I answered. "Like when we bark at strangers to keep the house secure."

"That reminds me," said Helen. "I still owe you for my citation."

I love being a cop!

With the smugglers behind bars, Wagstaff City was safe once again. At least, for a little while . . .

Part Two
MEET SPARKY

"Curious Crystal was in a pickle, all right! The 3:10 from Piscataway would be barreling down the tracks in a jiff. The girl detective was in trouble."

Helen stopped reading. "A detective is someone whose job is to find out things, like clues, to solve a mystery," she said.

Helen kept reading.

"*She gave Winky the secret danger whistle! Winky's ears went up. 'Bow wow!' he bellowed, and leapt out the window.*"

"Dogs don't go 'bow wow,'" I said. "We 'woof,' we 'arf,' we 'yip'—but 'bow wow'? I've never heard it."

"Martha, can't we finish the book?"

"Go on. I'm loving it," I said. "I'm on the edge of my tail."

"Winky raced to the train tracks, chewed through the ropes, and freed Curious Crystal! They hightailed it to the police station with the evidence. In minutes, Inspector Pinkus had caught Carnation Kelly red-handed! Curious Crystal and Winky had put a stop to the Carnation Caper!"

Helen closed the book. "The end."

"I don't get it," I said. "That Kelly guy was stealing capes? I thought he was after the diamonds."

"Not a cape. A caper," said Helen, lifting a box of books onto her bed. "A caper is a plan to try to steal something or commit a crime. Each of these books is about a different caper. *Curious Crystal and the Emerald Crab Caper, Curious Crystal and the Mysterious Cottage Caper . . .*"

She stared at the covers. "I wish I were a kid who solved mysteries."

"You'd be great!" I said. "You could be Heroic Helen and I'd be Sparky, your crime-sniffing sidekick."

"Okay," said Helen. "But first we need a mystery, Sparky."

I suggested we try the kitchen first. The mysteries would taste better.

"Look for anything strange and I'll write it down," she said.

I stopped in my tracks. "Look at that calendar! Tomorrow's date is circled in red!"

"So?" said Helen.

"It could be the date a crime is going to be committed. By . . . the Red Heart Gang!"

"That's *our* calendar," said Helen. "I don't think any criminals use our calendar to plan their crimes."

Then I noticed a tastier clue. "Crumbs! Let's follow them."

I licked them up as I went. Mmm. Detective work is delicious!

"Martha," said Helen, "there are no mysteries here. And even if there were, you'd be eating the evidence."

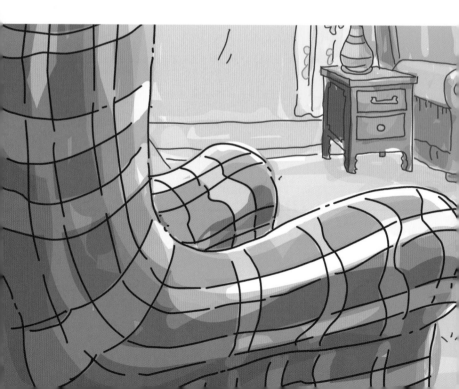

"I'm trying to find out what the criminal stole," I said, licking my chops. "I think it's apple cobbler."

The trail ended at my chair. "Aha! And the master thief was sitting in my chair— Oh!" I giggled, remembering my morning snack. "Actually, it was peach cobbler."

"Let's go outside before we discover what else the master thief stole," Helen suggested.

THE WHISTLER'S WARNING

"Hey, this might be something!" said Helen, picking a business card off the sidewalk. "Someone must have dropped it."

On the card was a picture of a top hat, mustache, and monocle, as well as a name. "The Whistler," read Helen. "Who do you think that is?"

"Someone who whistles?" I asked.

Helen flipped over the card and gasped.

I ran in panicked circles. "Who's been warned? Are *we* being warned? What about? What's going to happen to us?"

"Beats me. But Heroic Helen and Sparky are going to find out."

"Do we have to?" I asked.

"Yes," said Helen, examining the card. "The handwriting is distinctive. This is our first clue."

You've Been Warned !!

While she slipped it into her notebook, I sniffed a trail of muddy footprints on the sidewalk. "Is this another clue?" I asked.

"Weird," said Helen. "There's only the print of the right shoe. It's almost as if whoever made it was hopping."

"Maybe the Whistler is a hopper!" I said.

"Whoever made this footprint is going that way," said Helen. "Let's pursue it, Sparky!"

"W-w-wait a minute," I said, shuddering. "That footprint is huge. It could be a monster! Can't we pursue the hopping Whistler from home?"

"That wouldn't be a pursuit," said Helen. "If you pursue someone, you follow them so you can catch them."

"Okay," I said. "But I liked it better when we were pursuing the peach cobbler."

Helen and I followed the prints until they grew too faint to see. "The mud must be wearing off the sole," she sighed. "We've lost the trail."

Suddenly, we heard a loud, squelchy *THUD!*
It sounded like a giant. A *hopping* giant!

"It's him!" Helen shouted. "Hide!"

We dove into the bushes.

THUD! THUD! THUD!

"He's getting closer!" I whispered. My heart
beat faster as I imagined the one-footed giant
stomping us flat. Slowly, we peeked out of
the bushes.

"T.D.!" Helen cried.

"Aaaagh!" yelled T.D. as we popped out of the bushes.

"Aha!" I said. "*You* were making the footprint, so you're the Whistler! Who are you warning and what are you warning them about?"

"Huh?" he said.

"He's not the Whistler," said Helen. "T.D., what are you doing with that thing?"

"I got this mop stuck in my dad's boot," he said. "I thought walking around might loosen it up. Here, give me a hand."

"Nggh!" groaned T.D., straining in effort. "Who's the Whistler, anyway?"

"We don't know yet," I said. "We're going to find out."

POP! The boot came off, sending T.D. and Helen flying onto their bottoms. Mud splattered everywhere.

"Yeah," said Helen, frowning at her mud-soaked pants. "Right after Heroic Helen changes her clothes."

THE MYSTERIOUS MAN

Helen crossed out something in her notebook:

"There goes that clue," she said. "It was a red herring."

I raised my head from the water bowl. "Red herring?" I said. "I thought it was a mop in a boot."

"A red herring is something that throws detectives off the trail. It seems like a clue, but it's not."

"How many clues do we have left in the notebook?" I asked.

"Just one," said Helen, pulling out the business card. "There's no way we're going to find out who the Whistler is from this."

"Something's bound to turn up," I said.

Helen picked a piece of paper off the ground. "Litter!" she muttered. "People should clean up after themselves."

Then she read it. "Hey, it's a list of stores!"

"Flower shop," read Helen. "That's where Mom works! And this handwriting looks familiar."

Just then, a gloved hand reached out and snatched the list. A man with a thin mustache towered over us. He wore a suit with a carnation tucked into his lapel.

"Excuse me," he said. "But I believe that is mine. I dropped it when I was getting a yogurt."

The mysterious man turned to leave, but stopped. "Do you happen to know the way to the flower shop?" he asked.

"It's two blocks down and make a left," I told him.

"A talking dog," he murmured. "How curious. Much obliged." Then he put on his top hat and walked away.

Helen stared after him. "Martha!" she cried. "When was the last time you saw someone wearing a monocle and top hat in Wagstaff City?"

"Well, there's that guy on the peanut jar, and then there's that card we found—" I gasped. "He could be the Whistler!"

"Let's follow him!" said Helen.

But the man had vanished.

"He must be headed to the flower shop," said Helen. "If we hurry, we can beat him there."

Heroic Helen and Sparky took off in hot pursuit.

THE GENTLEMAN

At the flower shop, Helen and I hid behind large vases of flowers. "This is the perfect camouflage," she whispered.

"Huh?" I said.

"Camouflage is something you use to hide by blending into your background," she explained.

I nodded. "The Whistler will *never* find us—"

Just then, Mom gathered a bunch of our camouflage to fill an order.

"Mom, you're ruining our stake-out!" Helen said.

"Steak? Out?" I asked, popping up. "Steak out where?"

Helen giggled. "A stakeout is when you hide and wait for someone to show up so you can see what they're doing. Like if they're up to no good.

"Mom," she said. "We need to have a stakeout if we're going to catch a criminal."

"What criminal?" Mom asked.

"He wears a top hat and monocle and he's called the Whistler," I said.

Mom smiled. "Ooh, he sounds terrifying!"

"We're not positive he's a criminal," I said, "but he did want to know where the flower shop was."

"Well," said Mom, "if a man in a top hat and monocle comes by and tries to whistle at me, I'll let you know. In the meantime, could you pick up a chicken for dinner tomorrow?"

Helen wasn't happy about taking a break from our stakeout. But I suggested we move it to Karl's Butcher Shop and have real steak with it.

Sadly, that didn't happen. But Karl did toss me some brisket for being his last customer. "I'll lock up behind you," he said, following us to the door. "Since those recent robberies in the neighborhood, you can't be too careful."

"Robberies?" I asked. "What robberies?"

"Didn't you hear?" said Karl. "The dry cleaner, grocery store . . . I was robbed last week. And it was right after my birthday, too. Talk about a birthday surprise."

"Do the police have any idea who it might be?" asked Helen.

"No," said Karl. "But they're calling him the Gentleman. A witness said that the robber was very well dressed."

Then he waved goodbye and locked up.

"Whew!" I said. "I was afraid Karl was going to say that they're looking for someone called the Whistler."

"But what if the Whistler *is* the Gentleman?" said Helen. "He was well dressed, remember? Hmm. This is all going in the notebook. I just know that guy is up to something."

A SOGGY STAKEOUT

The next day, it rained on cats and dogs. Helen and I kept an eye on the flower shop from across the street. We hid behind some bushes.

"Why can't we have the stakeout inside like we did yesterday?" I asked.

"It's easier to run to the police from here," said Helen. "As soon as we see him, you hotfoot it to the station."

Her eyes widened. *"There he is!"*

The Whistler stopped outside the store.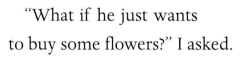

"What if he just wants to buy some flowers?" I asked.

"Then why isn't he going inside?" Helen said.

We watched him whip out his pocket watch, accidentally sending a sheet of paper to the sidewalk. Forget calling him the Whistler. He was more like Professor Butterfingers.

He peeked into the store window. As soon as Mom appeared, he ducked and darted away.

"Okay, that did look suspicious," I admitted.

"He must have thought that Mom saw him," Helen said. "I bet he comes back later. Now's our chance. Get the police!"

"I'm on it!" I said.

I beat paws to the station while Helen went to tell Mom that help was coming. On the way, she picked up the paper that the Whistler had dropped. It was sheet music.

"You've been warned!" read Helen. "Music and lyrics by Mack Guffin. Huh?"

"Helen!" called her Dad.

She looked up to see him.

"What are you doing here?" he asked nervously. "Mr. Guffin hasn't shown up yet, has he?"

"Mr. Guffin? Who's that?" asked Helen.

"I'd show you his card, but I lost it."

"Is this it?" asked Helen, holding up the Whistler's card.

"You found it!" Dad exclaimed. He peered into the shop window before whispering, "It's an anniversary surprise. I don't want your mother to see us."

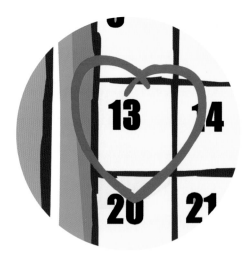

"So that's why there was a red heart on the calendar!" said Helen.

Meanwhile, I was at the police station.

"Let me get this straight," said the chief. "A man in a top hat and monocle named the Whistler is planning to rob the flower shop?"

"Right," I said. "Although he could also be calling himself the Gentleman."

"The Gentleman, eh?" said the chief. "And why should we take your word for this?"

"Because I helped you put away Louie Kablooie and Jimmy Gimme Moore? And the spy ring with those crooks who broke into the museum? And the rutabaga smugglers and— Seriously, do I really have to go through this every time?"

The chief turned to Officer O'Reilly. "She's got a point," he said. "All right, we'll check it out."

THE CROONING CROOK CAPER

While I was convincing the chief and Officer O'Reilly that something funny was going on at the flower shop, Helen was still there, talking to the Whistler.

"I hope we didn't mess things up," she said, handing him his sheet music.

He smiled. "Not at all. I had no idea I was being followed. You're quite the detective," he said. "Well, time to work."

"Can I help you with something?" Mom asked.

"Are you Mariela Lorraine?" asked the Whistler.

"Yes," Mom answered.

He opened his mouth to sing. The chief and I arrived just at that moment, but Helen blocked us at the door. "Wait," she whispered before Officer O'Reilly could say a word. "It's just a surprise for Mom, not a robbery."

Dad gave the Whistler the thumbs-up. At last, the Whistler began to sing.

"Your love I shall pursue," he crooned to Mom. "I'll stick to you like glue. Darling, you've been warned!"

Then he whistled a tune and ended with "Happy anniversary!"

Mom ran into Dad's arms. "Oh, Danny!" she cried. "You remembered!"

"See?" said the chief. "It's just a man who delivers singing telegrams."

"Wait a minute," said Helen, opening her notebook. "Could you tell me what stores have been robbed recently?"

The Chief listed them. "The butcher shop, the grocery store, and the dry cleaner. Why?"

"Did someone in all those places recently celebrate something, like a birthday?" Helen asked.

He shrugged. "You got me."

"Well," said Helen, "Karl at the butcher shop had a birthday. I wonder if he and the other stores got singing telegrams the day they were robbed. I think the Whistler *is* the Gentleman!"

"Hey, look!" I cried, spotting him. "He's unlocking the window!"

"That's how he did it!" said Helen. "He opened the windows at all the stores while he was delivering singing telegrams, so he could break in later!"

The Whistler made a mad dash for the door. But I beat him to it. *Grr,* I growled. "POLICE! FREEZE!"

A little while later, the Whistler was singing a new tune—the jailhouse blues.

"Oh, drat," he said, as the cell doors slammed on him.

"Well, Helen, you were right," said Officer O'Reilly.

"It was the handwriting that tipped me off," she said. "This is what the Whistler gave Dad to tell him what song he was going to sing for Mom's anniversary.

"And," she added, pointing to the Whistler's list of stores, "those are the places he robbed. The handwriting matches."

Officer O'Reilly shook her hand. "Great detective work, Helen!"

Case closed, we headed home. "We did it, Sparky," said Helen. "We solved the Crooning Crook Caper!"

"Bow wow, Heroic Helen," I said. "Bow wow."

GLOSSARY

How many words do you remember from the story?

beat: the route a police officer patrols

camouflage: what you wear to hide by blending into your background

caper: a plan to steal something or commit a crime

citation: a piece of paper that says someone broke the law

criminal: someone who commits a crime

detective: someone whose job is to discover clues to solve a mystery

monocle: an eyeglass for just one eye

patrol: to go around making sure everything is okay

pursue: to follow someone so you can catch them

security: actions taken to keep something safe

smuggle: to illegally sneak something into a place

stakeout: the act of hiding and waiting for people to show up so you can spy on them

Psst . . . What's the
Secret Word?

For this game, you'll need three players—a CLUE-GIVER and two DETECTIVES. Without showing the others, the clue-giver writes the vocabulary words on an index card. These are the secret words!

The clue-giver will offer a one-word clue for the detectives to guess the secret word. (The clue-giver may give up to five clues per word.) The first detective to guess correctly gets a point. The first detective to earn five points wins!

You Have the Right to
Remain Silent

Martha loves to talk . . . except when playing charades. Write the vocabulary words on small pieces of paper and divide them among the players. Without talking, take turns acting out the words. Each correct guess gets a point.

Police! Freeze!

Martha issues Helen a citation for speeding. Pretend you're a K-9 cop and create your own citations for family and friends. For example, you might give your brother a citation for wearing stinky socks. You can also design medals for good behavior. (Jelly doughnuts make good rewards too!)

Secret Agent Dog

Adaptation by Jamie White

Based on a TV series teleplay written by Ken Scarborough

Based on the characters created by Susan Meddaugh

Psst! **What you have in your hands is TOP SECRET.** It's about Secret Agent Martha, the talking dog.

Your mission, if you choose to accept it, is to read this book. Help Martha close a case! Crack a code! Uncover the meaning behind words like *scheme* and *mastermind*!

AGENT NAME: Martha

CODE NAME: K9-002

BODY TYPE: A dog of many parts
(medium-size mutt)

PAWPRINTS:

SPECIAL SKILL: The day Martha ate
alphabet soup, the letters in the soup
went to her brain instead of her
stomach. This mysterious event gave her
the gift of Human speech. Martha claims
that a bowl of Granny's Alphabet Soup
every day maintains her unique skill.
Although this explanation may be hard
to swallow, we can confirm that Martha
does speak Human . . . a lot!

METHOD OF OPERATION: Martha employs
her special speaking skills to solve

all sorts of crimes. One night when a burglar broke into her house, she called 911 and saved the day. On other occasions, she has corrected incomplete orders at the Burger Barn that otherwise would have left her burger-less. That would have been a crime!

FAMILY: Helen, baby Jake, Mom, Dad, and nontalking dog, Skits. (Sometimes Martha's family wishes she didn't talk *quite* so much. But who can argue with a talking dog?)

KNOWN ACCOMPLICES: Neighborhood dogs and Helen's best human friends—T.D., Alice, and Truman

ENEMIES: Most cats

RESIDENCE: Wagstaff City

OTHER: Martha enjoys hogging the sofa, controlling the TV remote, drinking toilet water, and of course TALKING! She dislikes baths and fleas.

Now that you've boned up on the facts about Martha, read her story. Dig up clues to solve the mystery. Good luck!

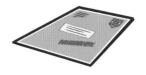

MARTHA, PLAIN MARTHA

Sometimes you don't need to look for adventure. Sometimes adventure finds you. That's what happened to me, Martha.

A few days ago, I was just minding my own business. Helen and I played fetch. T.D. watched us from our porch.

"Here you go," I said, dropping the stick at Helen's feet.

She threw it again. Ho-hum. Humans sure love throwing sticks. But I was bored.

"Aren't you going to fetch it?" asked Helen. "You were really excited about it a minute ago."

"Eh," I said. "I guess I've figured out how it works."

T.D. sighed. "Me, too."

"What do you want to do?" asked Helen.

"Can't we do something adventurous?" I said.

"Good idea!" said T.D.

"You have to go out and find adventure," said Helen. "You can't just expect it to come to you."

At that moment, a black car pulled up to the curb. Two people wearing dark sunglasses stepped out.

"Is one of you the talking dog?" asked the man.

I looked to my left and then to my right. No other dogs.

"Um . . . me?" I said.

"For you," said the woman, handing me an envelope.

Then they left. Just like that.

"What was that about?" I said. Or tried to say. It's hard to speak with an envelope in your mouth. Helen took it from me.

"Maybe it's an invitation to a surprise party," said T.D.

"I don't think so," I said. "I've never seen those guys before."

"Maybe that's the surprise," said T.D.

Helen opened the envelope. She read the letter aloud.

Dear Talking Dog,
Have you ever thought about becoming a secret agent?

"Martha? A secret agent?" T.D. said. "That would be perfect for you. You'll look like a normal dog, but you'll be fighting crime!"

"Cool," I said. "But what's a secret agent?"

"A secret agent is someone who does secret work," said T.D. "Like a spy."

A spy! I could just picture it. I'd wear a tuxedo and a tiara. Jazzy music would play wherever I went. I'd sneak into swanky places like casinos.

"I don't believe we've met," a man at my table would say.

"Martha," I'd introduce myself. "Plain Martha."

A waitress would serve me a drink. "For you. Fresh toilet water."

"Shaken, not stirred?" I'd ask. But then—
"*Wait!*" I'd say, knocking the dish off the table. "I didn't order a drink."

Splash! The spilled liquid would sizzle
and smoke.

"Bring me another one," I'd order. "But this
time, *hold the poison.*"

T.D. interrupted my daydream. "And if the
bad guys grab your collar, it could turn into
handcuffs and trap them!"

"You could have a doghouse that turns into
a car!" Helen added.

I was excited!

"So where do I go?" I asked.

Helen read from the letter:

> 131 Jones Street. Ask for the Chief.

A SOUP-ER MISSION

"This can't be right," I said. One thirty-one Jones Street didn't look like a spy agency. It looked like an auto body shop.

Clank! Bang! Clatter!

"EXCUSE ME!" I shouted to a mechanic. "I'm looking for the Chief."

He pointed toward a door in the back of the shop. I poked my head in and said, "Hellooooooooo?"

In his office, the Chief was sipping tea from behind a big desk. "Yes?"

"I'm Martha. The talking dog?"

"Ah, wonderful!" said the Chief. He stood up. "Come in. I'm glad you decided to lend us your services."

"Services?" I asked, taking a seat on the rug. "I thought you wanted me to work for you."

"Services are the jobs people, and sometimes dogs, do for other people," said the Chief. "In this job, your service will be to help us stop a terrible crime."

224

The Chief walked to a slide projector. He pressed a button. *Click!* A photo of a factory appeared on a screen. "I think you know this place."

"Granny's Soup Factory!" I exclaimed. Granny Flo made the alphabet soup that allowed me to speak.

"We have reason to believe that someone is trying to steal the formula for Granny's soup."

Click! Cans of soup popped up on the screen.

"The FORMULA FOR HER SOUP!" I cried. "That's horrible. *Who* would do that?"

"Well—"

"Wait!" I said. "What's a formula?"

"A formula is a recipe for something," the Chief explained. "The formula for the soup is Granny's secret list of ingredients. If another soup company stole the formula, they could put Granny out of business."

I gasped. "No more alphabet soup?"

I couldn't imagine life without speaking. How would I express my opinions? Talk on the phone? *Order pizza?*

"That's right," he said. "We need a secret agent to find out who is trying to steal the formula. And I must warn you, it might be dangerous."

Dangerous shmangerous.

"Let me at them," I said.

IT'S K9-002!

The Chief and I took a limo to Granny's Soup
Factory. I felt almost like a real secret agent.
But I was missing the best part.

"What about my disguise?" I asked. "I
could wear a tux."

"You don't need a disguise,"
said the Chief. "You have the
best disguise of all. No one
will ever suspect that a dog is
actually Secret Agent K9-002.
That's your new code name."

I tried it out. "K9-002! Watch out, it's K9-002!" It was no tux, but I liked the sound of it.

The limo arrived at the factory and we went inside.

Granny paced her office.

"I don't know what the fuss is about," she said. "No one could steal my secret formula. It's locked up in here." She moved a portrait of Granny Elsie, the company's founder, to reveal a safe. "I'm the only one who knows the combination. Trust me. No one can get to my soup formula."

"It would be difficult," the Chief agreed. "But these spies are tricky. If they ever got your formula, you'd be ruined."

Granny thought it over. "Well, as long as I don't have to pay for the guard dogs, I suppose there's no harm."

The Chief smiled as we left Granny's office.

"What did Granny mean when she said 'dogs'?" I asked. "Is there more than just—"

GRRR!

"Yow!" I yelped. I stood wet nose to wet nose with a mean-looking mutt. "Don't do that. You could really scare someone."

He growled again. *Yum!* I thought. *Someone* had been eating sausages.

"Martha, I'd like you to meet our other undercover agent, K9-001," said the Chief.

RUFF!

"Of course I'm not a spy," I answered. "As if!"

"K9-001 is one of our best secret agents. Have you seen anything out of the ordinary today, K9-001?"

RUFF! RUFF!

"What did he say?" the Chief asked me.

"He said 'nothing out of the ordinary.' But he thinks something will happen tonight."

"Well, K9-002, then it's up to you," said the Chief. "You're working tonight. Watch out for anything suspicious."

That night I reported for duty. The factory sure looked spooky in the dark. In the halls, I tried out my spy moves. I looked to the left. I looked to the right. I spun around.

Nothing.

I checked out the locker room. My ears stood up at the sound of a click. Somebody was unlocking the door!

The doorknob turned. A hand reached for the light switch. A shadowy figure stepped forward.

I gasped. *"YOU?"*

SOUP THIEF

"*Martha?*" asked T.D.

"What are you doing here?" we asked at the same time.

T.D.'s dad, O.G., stood with him, holding a toolbox.

"Hi, Martha," said O.G.

"I come here all the time with my dad. He works on the machines," said T.D. "The factory's cool at night."

"I'm sure glad it's you and not the soup thief," I said.

We followed O.G. to a machine.

"So you're doing surveillance?" T.D. whispered.

"No," I whispered. "I'm watching the factory."

"That's what *surveillance* means," said T.D. "It's when you watch really hard to see what someone is going to do or what will happen."

"Oh, surveillance!" I laughed. "I knew that. I thought you said . . . schmur . . . schmey . . . lance."

After asking permission from his dad, T.D. gave me a tour.

"I know every hiding place in this whole building," he said. "Watch this!" He pulled a book out of a bookcase. The bookcase swung out like a door. We stepped into a secret closet. Inside, a big window overlooked the factory floor.

"This is where Granny checks to see if everything is going okay," T.D. explained.

In the hall, something squeaked. *The soup thief!* I thought. T.D. and I peeked out.

"It's only the janitor," said T.D.

"We should watch him," I said. "Just to practice doing surveillance."

We watched the janitor stop in front of Granny's office. He took something out of his pocket, but it wasn't a key. He was picking the lock. Soon the door opened, and he was inside Granny's office.

The only thing that janitor wants to clean out is Granny's safe, I thought.

T.D. and I crept toward the office. We hid behind the janitor's cart and saw him looking through Granny's desk.

"What's he doing?" I whispered.

T.D. panicked. "He's coming this way!"

T.D. fled. I, uh, froze.

The janitor stuck his head into the hall. "Hello? Who's there?"

He looked right at me. YIKES! There was no talking my way out of this one. I'd have to rely on my good looks. I made my cutest face and wagged my tail.

"Ha!" laughed the janitor. "Some guard dog you are, pup."

But my tail wagged on as he walked away. *I'd found the soup thief!*

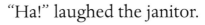

SOME RUFF NEWS

"Hang on," said O.G. "What happened?"

Back where we'd left O.G., T.D. and I told him about how we'd found the soup thief.

"I've got to tell the Chief," I said excitedly.

I ran to his office and waited there all night. When he arrived in the morning, I had a lot to say. I mean, even more than usual!

"The janitor?" said the Chief. "So that's their plan. Very good work, K9-002! We'd better warn Granny."

The Chief phoned her.

"The janitor?" said Granny. "That doesn't make sense. I think your secret agent is seeing things."

"Martha is one of our best agents," said the Chief. "You'd better make sure your formula is safe."

"Well, I suppose it couldn't hurt," she said. "Hang on." Granny closed her office door and bolted it. She checked her safe while K9-001 stood guard.

After a moment, the Chief hung up. "Granny says the formula is still safe in the, er, safe. Perhaps you fell asleep. You just dreamed that you saw the janitor."

"No!" I said. "He went into Granny's office. I wasn't the only one who saw him."

"Well, janitors *do* clean offices."

"By picking locks?" I asked. "I'm warning you, Chief. Something fishy is going on. I'm going to find out what it is!"

When I returned to the factory, I used my
sniffer to do some serious snooping. I tracked
the janitor to the locker room. He was on his
way out. I began to follow him, when—

GRR!

Yow! It was K9-001.

"I told you not to do that!" I scolded as the
janitor disappeared.

Ruff!

"You have a message for the Chief? What is it?"

Ruff!

"That makes no sense."

Ruff! Ruff!

"Oh, it's in code!"

I felt someone behind me. Slowly, I turned around. In the doorway, the janitor stared at me with his mouth wide open. UH-OH! I'd been caught red-pawed.

I fled the scene. I didn't stop running until I'd reached the Chief's office. (Do two-legged spies run this much? Where's my fancy car with the windows open and top down?) I delivered K9-001's message.

"November-29-X?" the Chief repeated.

"That's right. He said it was a code."

"It certainly is, Martha! The case is cracked. We have all the information we need to stop that spy." The Chief shook my paw. "Congratulations! You saved the soup!"

Yes! I went home to share the news with Helen and T.D.

"What a story!" said Helen. "You defeated the soup thief."

"Defeat?" I said. "Isn't that what you put in your shoes?"

Helen laughed. "No, *defeat* means to beat someone at something."

"I knew there was something sneaky about that janitor," said T.D. Just then, O.G. walked by.

"Dad!" T.D. called. "Where are you going? The factory is the other way."

"The factory is closed," said O.G.

"WHAT?" we asked.

"Someone stole the secret formula for the soup," he said. "And they say a dog helped them."

CRACKING
K9-002'S CODE

A dog helped someone steal Granny's secret formula? Impossible!

"That's what the other people who work at the factory said," said O.G. "Or at least, the people who *used* to work there."

"But how?" I asked. "It was locked up in the safe. No one had the combination except Granny."

O.G. sighed. "It looks like the bad guy got the combination somehow."

"We have to tell the Chief," I said.

I led them to his office. "This is it," I said when we reached the building. They didn't look so sure.

"*This* is the secret agent headquarters?" said O.G.

"Yes," I said. "Follow me."

O.G. looked around while Helen and T.D. followed me to the Chief's office. "Are you sure about this, Martha?" Helen asked.

"Yes! Come on!"

The Chief's door was open. I poked my head inside. But there was no Chief. There was no desk. There was nothing but boxes of junk!

"I'm telling you, there were carpets, drapes, and a desk," I said.

O.G. joined us. "I just talked to the manager. He says there was no spy agency here."

"But there was!" I insisted. "I was just here this morning. I gave the Chief the coded message from the other dog!"

"Uh-oh," said Helen.

"Uh-oh what?" I asked.

"I hope I'm wrong," said Helen, "but I think I know how the bad guys got the combination."

"How?" I asked.

"*You* told them."

"I did?"

"You didn't mean to. But think about it," said Helen. "You told the Chief about seeing the janitor. He had Granny check the safe. Then Granny locked the room so no one could see her. But she forgot about somebody."

"Huh?" I asked.

"The other dog gave you a coded message to give the Chief, right?" asked Helen.

"Holy hamburger!" I exclaimed. "K9-001 was the spy. He watched Granny put in the combination. So the coded message was actually the combination . . . November-29-X!"

But what did that mean? I put my doggy brain to work. I got nothing.

Then Helen said, "November is the *eleventh* month. *X* is the *twenty-fourth* letter of the alphabet. So the combination was . . ."

"*11-29-24!*" I said.

"And the Chief was actually . . ." O.G. began.

"The soup thief!" said the janitor. (You read that right. The janitor. He was standing in the doorway.)

"The janitor!" I cried. I leaped into a box. "HIDE!"

"Actually . . ." He ripped off his uniform to reveal a dark suit. "I'm Agent Johnson." He put on sunglasses and whipped out his badge. "I've been working undercover to defeat this gang of crooks. Looks like I'm too late."

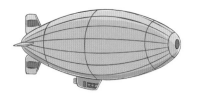

DOCTOR FELTMARKER

"You have to admit,"
said O.G. as we walked
home, "it was a clever
scheme."

"Scheme?" I said.
"You mean a sneaky plan
to do something bad?
That kind of scheme?
The kind I fell for?"

"Don't be so hard on
yourself," said Helen.

"Who would ever suspect a dog could be a spy?" said T.D.

"No one," said O.G. "That's what made it perfect. They pretended they were protecting Granny. But they had one problem. Their dog couldn't talk with the crook."

"Until I came along," I muttered. I'd wanted to be a secret agent so bad, I fell for it. Hook, line, and secret code.

At home, I moped on my chair.

"Come on, Martha," said Helen. "It's not really your fault."

"That's what you say. What if Granny doesn't make soup anymore? I won't be able to speak."

Helen turned off the light. "Don't worry, Martha. I'm sure Agent Johnson will catch those crooks."

I fell asleep. Until . . . *BRRRING!* The phone woke me late at night.

"Hello?" I answered it.

"It's Agent Johnson," said a deep voice. "We have a plan to get the formula back. But we need your help."

Agent Johnson told me his idea. The next day, I met him at a lab.

"Glad you could make it," said Agent Johnson. He introduced me to the Professor, the head of their operations.

"Pleased to meet you," said the Professor. He showed me a photo of the Chief and K9-001. "Are these the culprits?"

"Yes!" I said.

"Just as I thought," said the Professor. "The man you're looking for is a criminal mastermind. You know, a person who plans a complicated crime? His name is . . . *Doctor Feltmarker.*"

"He has a secret hideout," added Agent
Johnson. "No one has ever been able to find it."

"Here is a very rare picture of it," said the
Professor.

"The *sky?*" I asked, looking at a photo of
clouds.

"It's not just the sky. In the middle of the
picture is his hideout," he said. "It's an invisible
dirigible."

"An invisible dirigible?"

Agent Johnson nodded. "An invisible dirigible."

"An invisible dirigible. Very clever," I agreed. "Only . . . what's a dirigible?"

"It's a kind of giant balloon people fly around in," said the Professor. "But Feltmarker's dirigible is invisible. Here's what we think it looks like."

That's where I came in, they said. Dogs have an excellent sense of smell. I might not be able to see an invisible dirigible. But I could smell it.

"I'm happy to be of service," I said. "Just one question. That guy knows what I look like. Shouldn't I have a disguise?"

"Hmm. Not a bad idea," said the Professor.

I crossed my paws for a tux. But a moment later, I was wearing something VERY different.

"Not exactly the disguise I had in mind," I said. *Grr.*

"Well, very few dogs have a diamond collar," said the Professor.

IN THE INVISIBLE DIRIGIBLE

In his dirigible, the "Chief" put on his disguise. He drew a mustache on his face to become . . . the evil *Doctor Feltmarker!*

Feltmarker held up the soup formula. "My plan worked perfectly!" he laughed.

He had not only stolen Granny's formula.
He'd nabbed Granny, too! Nearby, she sat
trapped in a chair. K9-001, otherwise known
as Bruno, stood watch.

"The soup formula is ours! NOW WE'LL
CONTROL THE WORLD!" Feltmarker
cried. "Or, er, at least the soup world."

WOO! WOO! WOO! An alarm rang.

"What's that? Is something following us?" Feltmarker asked. He looked at a radar screen. A small dot blinked. "Too small to be a plane." He shrugged. "Bah, it's nothing!"

But it wasn't nothing. It was a flying pink poodle. Yes, it was yours truly. The Professor had strapped a flying pack to my back. Flying through the sky, I followed my nose to Feltmarker's hideout.

Sniff! "That's engine exhaust, all right," I said. "And it's coming from that dir—" *BONK!* My nose bounced off something hard. "Ha! Found it!"

Hovering over the hideout, I hit a switch on my pack strap. A gush of paint spurted out. Within seconds, the dirigible was no longer invisible. It was orange.

"Made it," I said, landing on the roof. "Flying pack off!"

The pack landed behind me. I slipped through the roof's small door. Inside, lights flashed.

"TRESPASSER ALERT! TRESPASSER ALERT!" said a robotic voice.

"Trespasser?" said Feltmarker.

"A trespasser is someone who has gotten inside who isn't allowed," said the computer.

"I know what a trespasser is!" he snapped. "Who's trespassing in my dirigible?"

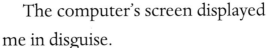

The computer's screen displayed me in disguise.

"A poodle? We'll see about that."

Feltmarker and Bruno hurried out of the control room to find me. Taking over the soup world would have to wait.

"Where are you?" Feltmarker called.

"Aha!" He bent down to inspect a trail of orange pawprints. "Whoever you are, you're smart enough to dump paint but not smart enough to keep from stepping in it!"

Feltmarker followed the tracks to a pink tail sticking out from around a corner. He grabbed for it.

"Got you!" he snarled.

HAPPY ITCHING!

Feltmarker held something up by the tail.
A pink poodle . . . *costume.* (Pretty sneaky
of me, eh?)

"A disguise?" he said.

While Feltmarker
puzzled over the
missing poodle,
I freed Granny.

"You saved me!"
she cried.

"No time for thanks," I said. "There's a
flying pack on top of the dirigible. Go for it!"

Granny ran for the door. At the last
moment, she turned back. "What about you?"

"I'll keep them busy while you escape. Hurry!"

As Granny raced off, I found the formula
and ate it. Blech. Not as tasty as the soup. I
gulped down the last of it just as Feltmarker
and Bruno burst in.

"Where is she?" Feltmarker said to himself.
"Where's Granny Flo?"

"Long gone, Feltmarker," I said, stepping
out from behind a chair.

"So it's you! I should have known."

"That's right. I'm sorry to inform you
that your little scheme didn't work. You're
defeated."

"Oh I am, am I?" Feltmarker
took a bone out of his pocket and
threw it at me. "Fetch, doggy!"

"Sorry, Feltmarker. But I'm in no mood for—" *Hiss.* Green mist rose from the bone and filled the air. "Sleeping . . . gas . . . zzz."

When I awoke minutes later, I found myself trapped in some kind of glass bubble.

"Where am I?" I murmured.

"Don't you know?" said Feltmarker. "You're in the *big time* now. Ha!"

It was true. I was in a huge hourglass. Feltmarker cranked its handle. The hourglass tipped.

Oof!—I fell to the bottom. Tiny black dots rained down on me.

"So you think you can bury me in sand, eh, Feltmarker?"

He cackled. "Oh, no. That isn't sand."

The sand hopped. It itched. It was . . . "FLEAS!" I cried.

"I'll be leaving you to have a good time with your friends," he said. "But don't worry. It won't be long."

Feltmarker turned to his control panel. "Computer, set for self-destruct!"

"Are you sure you want to self-destruct?" the computer asked. "Nothing will be saved. Press yes or cancel."

Feltmarker pressed a button. "Er, yes."

"*Self-destruct* means that something destroys itself, so that nothing is left. You *do* know that, don't you?" said the computer.

"Yes, yes."

"Self-destruct. Everything blows up. KERPOW!"

"Yes, yes, *YES!*"

"All right," said the computer. "Self-destruct in two minutes. Don't say I didn't warn you!"

"You'll never get away with it, Feltmarker!" I cried.

"I'm sorry," he said, strapping on a parachute vest. "I'd love to stay and chat, but I'm a little pressed for time."

Feltmarker and Bruno jumped out of the dirigible. "Happy itching!" he shouted.

Meanwhile, the computer counted down. 1:52 . . . 1:51 . . . 1:50 . . .

It looked hopeless. *Was there no fleeing Feltmarker's fleas?*

KERPOW!

Invisible dirigible. Say that three times fast.
It's almost as impossible as escaping from
one while trapped in an hourglass full of fleas.

The clock ticked on. 1:21 . . . 1:20 . . . 1:19 . . .

"I can't die wearing a
stinkin' diamond poodle
collar," I said.

Wait a minute, I thought.
*Diamonds! It's a good thing
Agent Johnson and the Professor
didn't skimp on my disguise.*

1:05 . . . 1:04 . . . 1:03 . . .

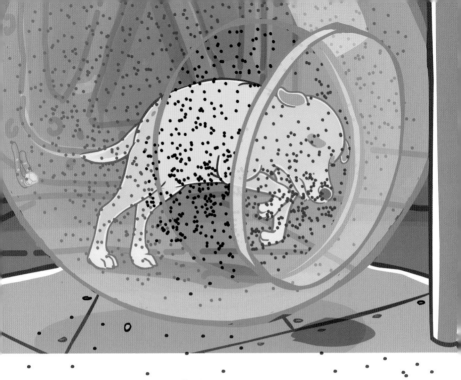

I yanked off the collar. Holding it with my teeth, I used the diamond to cut a circle in the glass. Then I pushed, and the glass fell out. (My coolest spy move yet!)

00:59 . . . 00:58 . . .

Oh, no. OH, NO. The place was seconds away from going KABOOM! I looked at the computer's buttons. One of them *had* to stop it!

If only I weren't so itchy. Argh! I scratched
and scratched. My paw accidentally hit a
button. Everything started blinking red.
Somehow I had a feeling that wasn't good.

"Ten seconds to self-destruct," said the
computer.

Yow! What do I do? What do I do? I ran back
and forth. "Pull yourself together, Martha," I
told myself. "After all, you are a secret agent."

"Five seconds," said the computer.

YOW! WHAT DO I DO? WHAT DO I DO?

"Martha!" a voice called.

Just outside the open door, Granny hovered in the air. She was wearing my flying pack.

"Jump!" she cried, holding out her arms.

I leaped, and we escaped, just as . . .
KERPOW! The dirigible exploded behind us.

"Whoa! That was close," I said.

"Look down below!" said Granny.

We floated toward the Come-On-Inn. I could already smell their sausages. *Mmm.* I love the smell of sausages.

"HELP! HELP! GET US DOWN!" someone shouted. Dangling from a tree were Feltmarker and Bruno. Granny and I flew over to them.

"It looks like you two decided the Come-On-Inn is a nice place to hang out," I said.

Feltmarker looked surprised. Then he looked . . . itchy. Lots of tiny black dots were falling onto his head.

"What is that?" he asked. "Rain?"

"No." I smiled. "Fleas."

"FLEAS? NO! GET ME OUT OF HERE!" hollered Feltmarker. "HELP!"

Granny and I landed as the bad guys scratched like crazy.

"You did it, Martha!" said Agent Johnson, suddenly appearing. "You saved the soup!"

Only . . . I didn't.

SAUSAGE BREATH

"Martha? Wake up," said Helen. "You're talking in your sleep."

I opened my eyes. "You mean I was just dreaming? I haven't really caught those crooks?"

"Sorry," said Helen.

Grr. I hate it when it all turns out to be a dream. As Helen made me soup, I told her all about it. "It made me hungry for sausages."

"Well, all we have is soup. And not much more of it if they don't catch those bad guys," said Helen.

"The funny thing is, I feel like I've smelled those Come-On-Inn sausages somewhere else recently. But where?"

Then it hit me like bad dog breath. "Sizzling sausages! I remember."

I raced out the door to get Agent Johnson. He followed me, and I followed my nose— straight to the Come-On-Inn.

We found the crooks just where I thought they'd be. At a table, they were gobbling up the best sausages in town. They sure looked shocked to see me again.

"It's over, Feltmarker—er, Chief!" I said.

And that's how we snagged the soup thieves. Granny's alphabet soup was SAVED!

"Great work, Martha," said Agent Johnson. "But how did you figure out where those crooks were hiding?"

"Simple. By using my sense of smell. I'd smelled sausages my first day on the job. It was the Chief's dog's breath. There's only one place in town that serves sausages with that delicious, tender, tasty . . ."

"I get it," said Agent Johnson.

"Sorry. With that nice sausage smell," I said. "But it wasn't until I had my dream that I remembered where those sausages came from. The Come-On-Inn! Then I knew this must be where those crooks were hiding."

"Your dream saved the soup recipe," said Agent Johnson. "I don't know how we can ever repay you."

"Well, I have a thought." I licked my lips.

Agent Johnson laughed. "Okay, Martha. The sausages are on me."

So there you have it. Thanks to my superduper sniffer, Granny's soup was back on the burner. Mission accomplished!

But bad guys, beware. You have not seen the last of . . . Martha. Plain Martha.

GLOSSARY

Ｈow many words do you remember from the story?

defeat: to beat someone at something, to win

formula: a recipe for something

mastermind: someone who plans a complicated project or activity

scheme: a sneaky plan, usually to do something bad

secret agent: someone who does secret work

self-destruct: to destroy oneself or itself

service: a job someone does for others

surveillance: to watch carefully to see what someone is going to do or what will happen

trespasser: someone who has entered a place without the owner's permission

Secret Message

To write secret messages to your friends, use K9-001's code or make up your own. You can create an invisible letter by using a white crayon on white paper. Make your message appear by coloring over it with a marker.

K9-001's Secret Code

1	2	3	4	5
A	B	C	D	E

6	7	8	9	10
F	G	H	I	J

11	12	13	14	15
K	L	M	N	O

16	17	18	19	20
P	Q	R	S	T

21	22	23	24	25
U	V	W	X	Y

26
Z

Martha Speaks
Martha's Super Spy Test

Psst. Do you want to be a secret agent like me? Then take my super spy test. To pass, crack the code of eight or more of the sentences below. (Hint: use K9-001's code from the story.)

1. To become a 13 - 1 - 19 - 20 - 5 - 18 - 13 - 9 - 14 - 4 , plan a big crime and perfect an evil laugh. Muwhahaha!

2. A cat in a dog park is a 20 - 18 - 5 - 19 - 16 - 1 - 19 - 19 - 5 - 18 .

3. My 6 - 15 - 18 - 13 - 21 - 12 - 1 for the perfect snack = sausage + sausage + sausage!

4. Feltmarker's 19 - 3 - 8 - 5 - 13 - 5 to steal the soup formula landed him in hot water.

5. My 19 - 5 - 18 - 22 - 9 - 3 - 5 - 19 include sniffing out lost shoes and garbage. Mmm!

6. No one can 4 - 5 - 6 - 5 - 1 - 20 Skits at catching flying objects.

7. When I did 19 - 21 - 18 - 22 - 5 - 9 - 12 - 12 - 1 - 14 - 3 - 5 in Granny's factory, I was *soup-rised* to see T.D.

8. If you pass this test, your code name—is

19 - 5 - 3 - 18 - 5 - 20   1 - 7 - 5 - 14 - 20 — 003!

9. Warning: this page will 19 - 5 - 12 - 6 — 4 - 5 - 19 - 20 - 18 - 21 - 3 - 20 in five seconds. (Just kidding!)

Master of
Disguise

A good spy blends into any surrounding. To create your own disguise, mix and match clothing and props. Try sunglasses, hats, scarves, uniforms, and long coats. Change your hairstyle. Use makeup to draw a mustache, wrinkles, or a black eye. No one will ever guess your true identity!